MW01226954

Mermaid Tales

AN AROUND THE WORLD MERMAID COLORING ADVENTURE!

by Deb Soromenho

*Don't forget to actually search the coordinates on a maps app!

Remarkably, spotted at night in the Red Sea, just off the coast of Africa

18°49'94" N, 39°57'18" E

Amazing manatee mermaid spotted in the Amazon River.   2°63'67" S, 56°97'60" W

A rare shark tail mermaid spotted in the Sydney Harbor, Australia

33.8523° S, 151.2108° E

Super rare Orca mermaid spotted from a fishing boat in the Bering Strait   66°61'11" N, 167°09'80" W

This flamboyant mermaid was potted playing in the warm waters of Rio, Brazil

22°94'26" S, 43°16'75" W

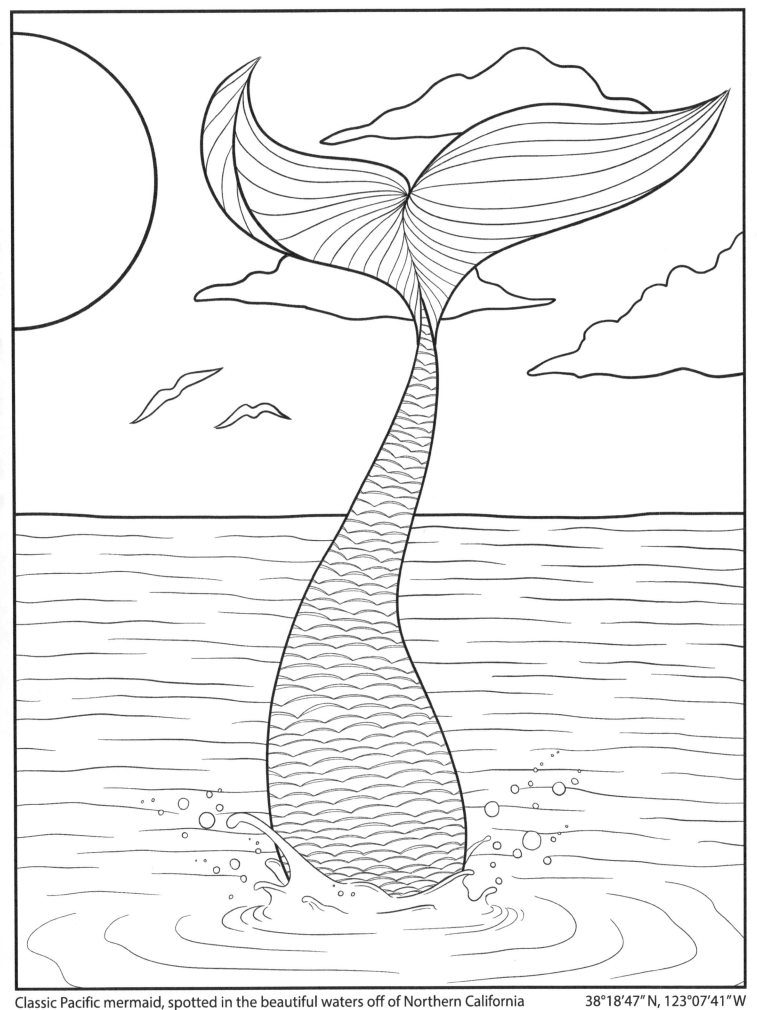

Classic Pacific mermaid, spotted in the beautiful waters off of Northern California   38°18'47" N, 123°07'41" W

Arctic mermaid spotted close to Vancouver in British Columbia, Canada   53°06'15" N, 130°50'60" W

Rare Dragon mermaid seen from a remote island in the South China Sea

10°47'40" N, 109°15'01" E

An actual Melusine mermaid seen from the Cliffs of Dover, England   51°13'13" N, 1°36'10" E

This beauty was potted just after sunrise off the Coast of Goa, India   15°04'35" N, 73°54'96" E

Such a graceful mermaid, she was seen splashing in the surf near Athens, Greece   37°89'67" N, 23°69'41" E

Beautiful Caribbean mermaid spotted from Havana, Cuba

23°22'61" N, 82°43'57" W

Mermaid with unusual markings seen just off the coast of the Big Island, Hawai'i   19°30'53" N, 156°05'20" W

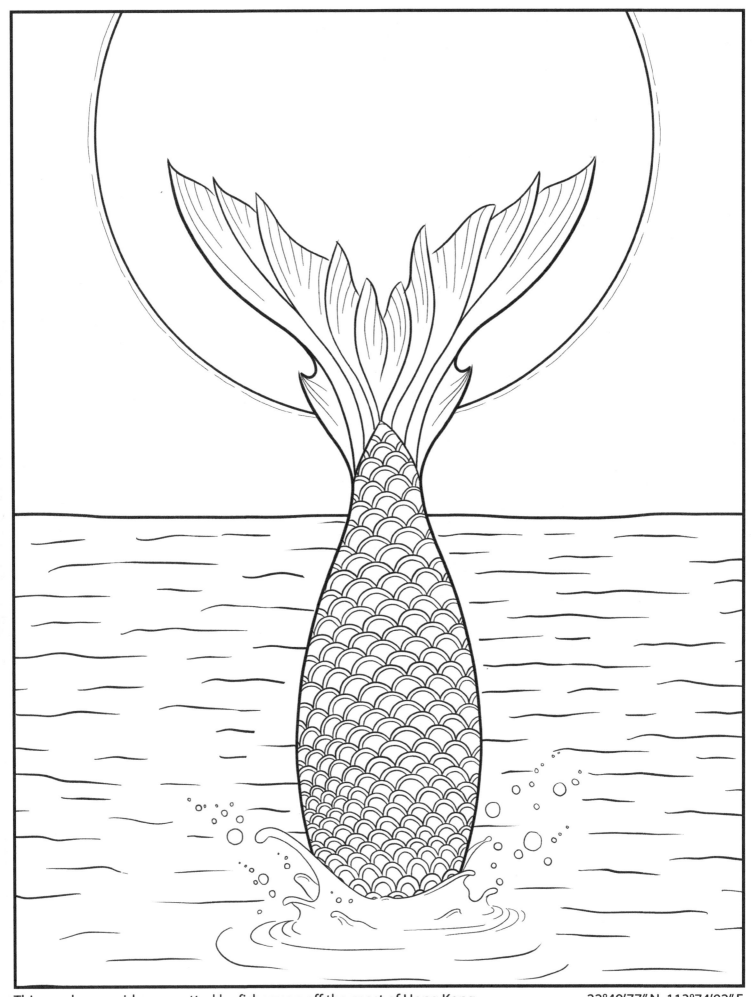

This regal mermaid was spotted by fisherman off the coast of Hong Kong

22°49'77" N, 113°74'92" E

This unusual mermaid was spied just off the coast of Reykjavik, Iceland

64°22'76" N, 22°19'54" W

Gorgeous tropical mermaid spotted just off shore in Montego Bay, Jamaica   18°54'58" N, 78°05'11" W

This gorgeous Koi mermaid was spotted offshore in Japan

34°08'32" N, 133°55'43" E

Spotted in the Indian Ocean, just off of Madagascar

20°34'71" S, 50°27'34" E

This beauty was spotted in the Malacca Strait, Malaysia

5°36'97"N, 98°96'57"E

Seen frolicking with dolphins off the west coast of Mexico, near Puerta Vallarta   21°02′01″N, 106°85′65″W

A true Viking mermaid spotted in the North Sea, off the Coast of Norway

57°59'16" N, 8°23'13" E

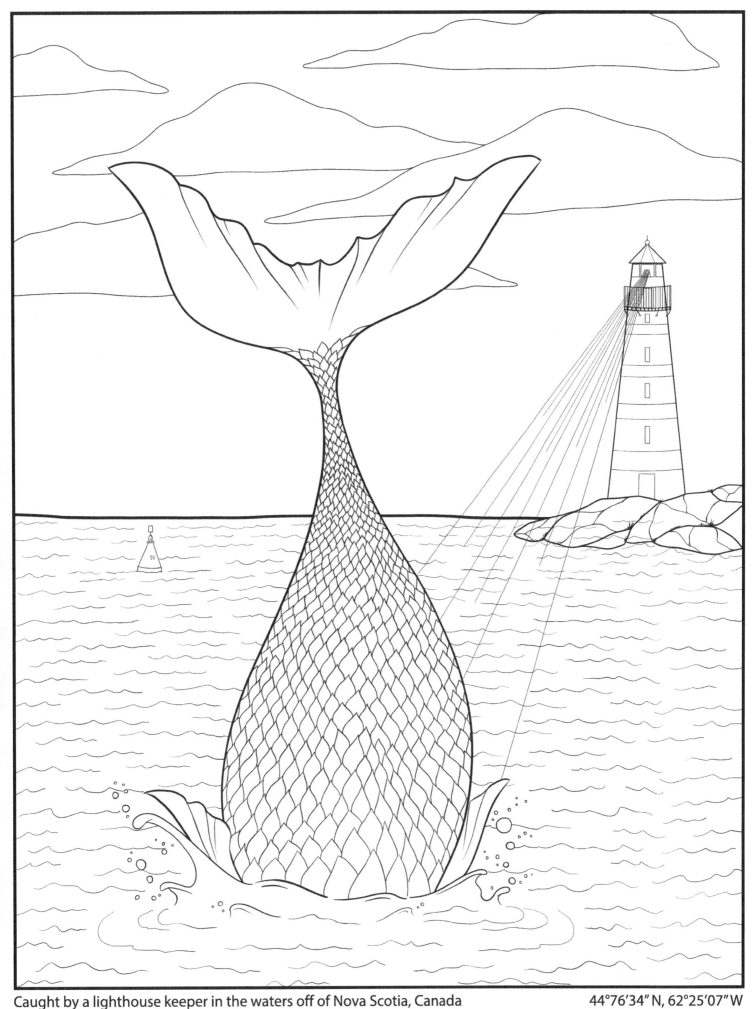

Caught by a lighthouse keeper in the waters off of Nova Scotia, Canada

44°76'34" N, 62°25'07" W

This exotic mermaid was spotted in the waters off of a remote Polynesian Island

3°94'37" S, 157°17'26" E

This ancient mermaid was spotted off the Coast of Southern Portugal 36°69'19" N, 8°07'84" W

Incredible Electric eel mermaid spotted in Maracaibo, Venezuela

9°71'42"N, 71°60'64"W

Mermaid Tales

by Deb Soromenho

All illustrations copyright © Deb Soromenho Art 2020
Do not reproduce illustrations or use for resale of any kind.

www.debsoromenho.com

Made in the USA
Middletown, DE
08 October 2022

12242784R00031